Henry's Secret Valentine

OTHER YOUNG YEARLING BOOKS YOU WILL ENJOY:

TOO MANY RABBITS, *Peggy Parish*
"BEE MY VALENTINE!", *Miriam Cohen*
LIAR, LIAR, PANTS ON FIRE!, *Miriam Cohen*
FIRST GRADE TAKES A TEST, *Miriam Cohen*
JIM'S DOG MUFFINS, *Miriam Cohen*
JIM MEETS THE THING, *Miriam Cohen*
SEE YOU TOMORROW, CHARLES, *Miriam Cohen*
STARRING FIRST GRADE, *Miriam Cohen*
MEET THE LINCOLN LIONS BAND, *Patricia Reilly Giff*
THE "JINGLE BELLS" JAM, *Patricia Reilly Gill*

YEARLING BOOKS/YOUNG YEARLINGS/YEARLING CLASSICS are designed especially to entertain and enlighten young people. Patricia Reilly Giff, consultant to this series, received her bachelor's degree from Marymount College and a master's degree in history from St. John's University. She holds a Professional Diploma in Reading and a Doctorate of Humane Letters from Hofstra University. She was a teacher and reading consultant for many years, and is the author of numerous books for young readers.

For a complete listing of all Yearling titles, write to
Dell Readers Service, P.O. Box 1045, South Holland, IL 60473.

Henry's Secret Valentine

written and illustrated
by
Jeffrey Dinardo

A Young Yearling Book

Published by
Dell Publishing
a division of
Bantam Doubleday Dell Publishing Group, Inc.
666 Fifth Avenue
New York, New York 10103

ISBN: 0-440-40758-3

Printed in the United States of America

February 1993

10 9 8 7 6 5 4 3 2 1

WES

To my wife, Kristine,
with love

Ms. Bird and her class were
making red hearts.
Valentine's Day was only three
days away and the class was
going to have a party.
Henry couldn't wait.

Aa Bb Cc Dd Ee
Valentine
1) Cut out
2) Color i
3) Do not
Ms. Bird

Simon hung
decorations
around the room.

Rich and Lisa
planned what
food to bring . . .

and everyone made valentines to
give to each other.

Henry passed the glue to Sarah.

"Thanks, Henry," she said.

Henry liked the way Sarah smiled.

I'm going to send her *two* valentines, he thought.

Just then someone new walked into the classroom. She handed a note to Ms. Bird.

Simon nudged Henry.

"Who's that?" he whispered.

"I don't know," said Henry, but he thought she looked scared.

"This is Frieda," Ms. Bird announced. "She just moved here and is joining our class. I hope you will all make her your friend."

SAVE
OUR

At recess Henry saw
Frieda standing by
herself.
"Hi, I'm Henry," he
said. "Do you want
to play catch?"

Frieda looked
down and didn't
say a word.

At lunchtime Henry offered
Frieda one of his oatmeal
cookies. Frieda just mumbled
and sipped her milk.
She must not like me,
Henry thought.
So he ate all the
cookies himself.

That night, Henry told his
parents about Frieda.
"She's probably shy," said
his mother.
"Remember how you felt your
first day at camp?" his father said.
"I was scared," said Henry.
"I didn't know anyone."

CAMP PINECONE

The next day at school
Henry watched as Ms. Bird
wrote on the blackboard.
"It's time for some math," she said.
"Please take out your books."

When Henry opened his book
something fell out.
It was big.
It was red.

It was a valentine!

It read:

Sarah whispered to Henry, "Do you have an extra eraser I can borrow?" Then she smiled at him. Henry's heart beat faster. Sarah must have sent me the valentine! he thought.

At noon, Henry opened his lunch box. Inside he found his favorite sandwich, peanut butter and banana.

Under it he found a surprise.

It was big.

It was red.

It was *another* valentine!

It read:

Henry smiled right at Sarah.

She smiled back.

The next day Sarah came running up to Henry.
"Hi, Henry," she said. "Would you do me a favor?"
"Anything!" he said.
Sarah took out a big valentine and gave it to him.

Henry quickly read it.

"Simon!" said Henry.

"Shhh!" said Sarah. "I want to surprise him. Would you put this in Simon's desk for me?"

Henry's beak trembled. Could Sarah be sending secret valentines to two friends? he thought. Or maybe she's not my secret valentine at all.

"Sure," he said sadly. "I'll take care of it."

Sarah

The rest of the morning Henry did not receive any more valentines. He checked all of his books twice.

At lunch he was sure he would find a new valentine in his lunch box.

But inside there was only a
tuna fish sandwich, a bag of chips,
and a pickle.

Henry waited and waited.
At the end of the day he sighed.
I guess I'm not getting any more
secret valentines, he thought.

When Henry went to get his coat
he saw a paw slipping something
into his boot.
It was big.
It was red.
It was a valentine!

Henry flung open the door.

It was Frieda!

"You gave me those valentines?"
Henry asked. "You don't even
know me!"

Frieda looked down.

"I don't know *anyone* since I
moved here," she whispered.
"But you were nice to me."

She grabbed her coat and ran
out of the classroom ahead of
the others.
Henry thought about Frieda.
He thought about his first day
at camp. And he had an idea.
He called his friends together
and told them his plan.
"That's a great idea," Sarah said.
The rest of the class agreed.

At the Valentine's Day party,
there were lots of valentines
for everyone.

"Look at the silly
one Rich sent me,"
said Sarah.

"Here's a robot
one from Henry,"
Simon said.

Ms. Bird got lots of valentines too.

But Frieda got the most!

Everyone in class had sent her

two valentines.

Frieda didn't stare at the ground.

She didn't mumble.

She jumped up and smiled.

"Thank you!" she said.

Ms. Bird brought out cupcakes
and fruit punch.
Then the class sang songs.
Frieda sang a funny song about
fish swimming in a pool.

Everyone laughed and clapped.

"We used to sing that at my old school," she said as she took a bow.

Henry thought she had a great smile.

At the end of the day everyone
put on their coats and boots.
Henry stood by the classroom
door and watched Frieda.
She put her arm in her sleeve
and found something!
It was big.
It was red.

It was one

last valentine!

It read:

FRIEDA
Oatmeal is lumpy
Ice cream is cool
I'm glad you're my friend
and came to this school
HENRY

The End

Jeffrey Dinardo has always loved to draw and write stories about animals. Henry has been waiting to have his own series of books for a long time, and a parade of other feathered and furry characters is sure to follow.

Jeff went to Skidmore College and now lives in Boston, Massachusetts, with his wife, Kristine, and their beagle, Jasmine, who was the model for Sarah. They also have two cockatiels who both modeled for Ms. Bird.

Turn the page to make
your very own valentine!

Follow these easy directions to make your own valentine

1) Draw a picture of a favorite friend in the center.
2) Color it the way you want.
3) Cut along the dotted line.
4) Don't forget to sign it!